BRANDON BEAR

WRITTEN BY

JOHN EMIL BECKER, PH.D.

ILLUSTRATIONS BY

ALEENA VALENTINE-LOPEZ

TO MY GRANDSON BRANDON WHO HAS ALWAYS LOVED SPORTS OF ALL KINDS

JOHN

DEDICATED TO MY YOUNGER SIBLINGS AND COUSINS, TO ALL CHILDREN AND OUR HAPPY CHILDHOOD MEMORIES.

ALEENA

BRANDON BEAR IS QUITE AN ACTIVE LITTLE BEAR.

HE LOVES TO RUN,

AND JUMP,

AND PLAY.

HE ESPECIALLY LIKES TO PLAY SPORTS
WITH HIS DADDY AND HIS GRANDPA.

BRANDON LOVES TO PLAY SOCCER.

HE IS GOOD AT PASSING THE BALL....

AND DRIBBLING THE BALL
WITH HIS FEET . . .

BRANDON
1

AND SCORING GOALS. HE REALLY LIKES
SCORING GOALS!

GRAN
2
BRANDON
1
DAD
3

BRANDON ALSO LOVES TO PLAY BASEBALL.

HE IS GOOD AT THROWING THE BALL . . .

AND CATCHING THE BALL . . .

AND HITTING THE BALL. HE REALLY LIKES
HITTING THE BALL!

GRANDPA
3
BRANDON
1

BRANDON ALSO LOVES TO PLAY
BASKETBALL.

HE IS GOOD AT DRIBBLING THE BALL . . .

AND PLAYING DEFENSE . . .

AND SHOOTING BASKETS. HE REALLY
LIKES SHOOTING BASKETS!

BRANDON ALSO LOVES TO PLAY
FOOTBALL.

BRA
BRANDON BEAR 1

HE IS GOOD AT RUNNING WITH THE BALL . . .

AND CATCHING PASSES . . .

AND SCORING TOUCHDOWNS. HE REALLY LIKES SCORING TOUCHDOWNS!

DAD
BRANDO
1

BRANDON ALSO LOVES TO PLAY TENNIS.

BRANDON
1
B
BRANDON BEAR 1

HE IS GOOD AT HITTING THE BALL AFTER
IT BOUNCES . . .

AND HITTING THE BALL IN THE AIR . . .

AND SERVING THE BALL. HE REALLY LIKES SERVING!

BUT MOST OF ALL, BRANDON LOVES TO PLAY HOCKEY.

HE REALLY, REALLY LOVES TO PLAY HOCKEY.

HE IS GOOD AT STICKHANDLING THE PUCK . . .

AND PASSING THE PUCK . . .

AND SHOOTING THE PUCK. HE REALLY, REALLY, LIKES SHOOTING THE PUCK INTO THE NET!

AND WHEN DADDY AND GRANDPA ARE
WORN OUT . . .

BRANDON BEAR GOES OFF TO FIND SOME OF HIS FRIENDS WHO ALSO LIKE TO PLAY SPORTS.

DR. JOHN EMIL BECKER IS AN AUTHOR OF 28 CHILDREN'S BOOKS INCLUDING HIS FICTIONAL PICTURE BOOKS, MAGGIE THE TALENTED MOUSE, AND MUGAMBI'S JOURNEY, HIS BEST-SELLING BOOK, FRENEMIES FOR LIFE, THE MULTIPLE AWARD-WINNING BOOK, WILD CATS PAST & PRESENT, THE RETURNING WILDLIFE SERIES, AND EIGHT SEEDLING BOOKS. HE IS A GRADUATE OF THE OHIO STATE UNIVERSITY, A FORMER ELEMENTARY SCHOOL TEACHER, COLLEGE PROFESSOR AT MACALESTER COLLEGE AND THE UNIVERSITY OF FLORIDA, ADMINISTRATOR AT THE COLUMBUS ZOO, AND HE WORKED IN THE FIELD OF WILDLIFE CONSERVATION FOR MANY YEARS. DR. BECKER ALSO TAUGHT WRITING AT THE THURBER HOUSE LITERARY CENTER IN COLUMBUS, OHIO, FOR TWENTY YEARS. HE CURRENTLY LIVES IN DEERFIELD BEACH, FLORIDA. YOU MAY CONTACT DR. BECKER THROUGH HIS WEBSITE: WWW.JOHNBECKERAUTHOR.COM.

BORN AND RAISED IN SOUTH FLORIDA, ALEENA VALENTINE-LOPEZ IS A SELF-TAUGHT ARTIST WHO SPECIALIZES IN CHARACTER DESIGN AND STORYTELLING. WITH A BACKGROUND IN MARINE BIOLOGY AND CRIMINAL JUSTICE, HER PASSION FOR ART STEMS FROM A LOVE OF COMIC BOOK STORYTELLING AND HAND-DRAWN ANIMATIONS. SHE HAS WORKED AS AN ILLUSTRATOR FOR INDEPENDENT PUBLISHING COMPANIES SUCH AS BOLD ADVENTURE PRESS AND ZORRO PRODUCTION, AS WELL AS PRIVATE COMMISSIONS.